This edition published in 1991 by SMITHMARK Publishers Inc., 112 Madison Avenue, New York, NY 10016.

SMITHMARK books are available for bulk purchase for sales promotion and premium use. For details, write or telephone the
Manager of Special Sales, SMITHMARK Publishers Inc., 112 Madison Avenue, New York, NY 10016. (212) 532-6600.

Jim Henson's Muppet Babies'

CHRISTMAS BOOK

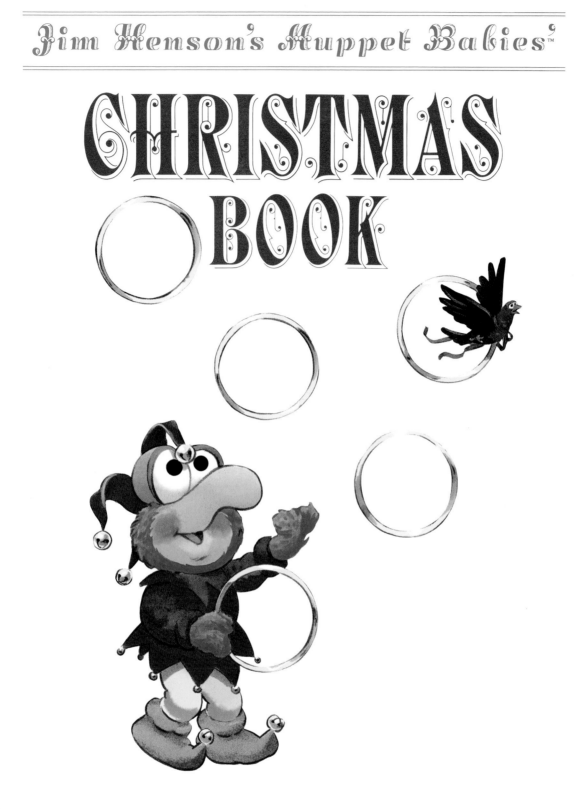

illustrated by Tom Brannon

◆

Muppet Press

SMITHMARK

THE TWELVE DAYS OF CHRISTMAS

On the first day of Christmas,
my true love gave to me

A partridge in a pear tree.

On the second day of Christmas,
    my true love gave to me

Two turtle doves
And a partridge in a pear tree.

On the third day of Christmas,
my true love gave to me

Three French hens,
Two turtle doves,
And a partridge in a pear tree.

On the fourth day of Christmas,
   my true love gave to me

Four calling birds,
Three French hens,
Two turtle doves,
And a partridge in a pear tree.

On the fifth day of Christmas,
  my true love gave to me

Five gold rings,
Four calling birds,
Three French hens,
Two turtle doves,
And a partridge in a pear tree.

On the sixth day of Christmas,
    my true love gave to me

Six geese a-laying,
Five gold rings,
Four calling birds,
Three French hens,
Two turtle doves,
And a partridge in a pear tree.

On the seventh day of Christmas,
    my true love gave to me

Seven swans a-swimming,
Six geese a-laying,
Five gold rings,
Four calling birds,
Three French hens,
Two turtle doves,
And a partridge in a pear tree.

On the eighth day of Christmas,
   my true love gave to me

Eight maids a-milking,
Seven swans a-swimming,
Six geese a-laying,
Five gold rings,
Four calling birds,
Three French hens,
Two turtle doves,
And a partridge in a pear tree.

On the ninth day of Christmas,
    my true love gave to me

Nine ladies dancing,
Eight maids a-milking,
Seven swans a-swimming,
Six geese a-laying,
Five gold rings,
Four calling birds,
Three French hens,
Two turtle doves,
And a partridge in a pear tree.

On the tenth day of Christmas,
my true love gave to me

Ten lords a-leaping,
Nine ladies dancing,
Eight maids a-milking,
Seven swans a-swimming,
Six geese a-laying,
Five gold rings,
Four calling birds,
Three French hens,
Two turtle doves,
And a partridge in a pear tree.

On the eleventh day of Christmas,
  my true love gave to me

Eleven pipers piping,
Ten lords a-leaping,
Nine ladies dancing,
Eight maids a-milking,
Seven swans a-swimming,
Six geese a-laying,
Five gold rings,
Four calling birds,
Three French hens,
Two turtle doves,
And a partridge in a pear tree.

On the twelfth day of Christmas,
    my true love gave to me

Twelve drummers drumming,
Eleven pipers piping,
Ten lords a-leaping,
Nine ladies dancing,
Eight maids a-milking,
Seven swans a-swimming,
Six geese a-laying,
Five gold rings,
Four calling birds,
Three French hens,
Two turtle doves,

And a partridge in a pear tree.

THE NIGHT BEFORE CHRISTMAS

'Twas the night before Christmas,
When all through the house
Not a creature was stirring,
Not even a mouse.

The stockings were hung
By the chimney with care,
In hopes that Saint Nicholas
Soon would be there.

The children were nestled
All snug in their beds,
While visions of sugarplums
Danced in their heads.

And Mama in her kerchief
And I in my cap
Had just settled down
For a long winter's nap.

When out on the lawn
There arose such a clatter,
I sprang from my bed
To see what was the matter.

Away to the window
I flew like a flash,
Tore open the shutters,
And threw up the sash.

When what to my wondering
Eyes should appear,
But a miniature sleigh
And eight tiny reindeer,

With a little old driver,
So lively and quick,
I knew in a moment
It must be Saint Nick.

More rapid than eagles
His coursers they came,
And he whistled and shouted,
And called them by name:

"Now, Dasher! Now, Dancer!
Now, Prancer and Vixen!
On, Comet! On, Cupid!
On, Donder and Blitzen!

"To the top of the porch!
To the top of the wall!
Now dash away! Dash away!
Dash away all!"

So up to the housetop
The coursers they flew,
With the sleigh full of toys
And Saint Nicholas, too.

And then in a twinkling,
I heard on the roof,
The prancing and pawing
Of each little hoof—

As I drew in my head
And was turning around,
Down the chimney Saint Nicholas
Came with a bound.

A bundle of toys
He had flung on his back,
And he looked like a peddler
Just opening his pack.

His eyes—how they twinkled!
His dimples, how merry!
His cheeks were like roses,
His nose like a cherry!

He had a broad face
And a little round belly
That shook when he laughed,
Like a bowlful of jelly.

He was chubby and plump,
A right jolly old elf,
And I laughed when I saw him,
In spite of myself.

A wink of an eye
And a twist of his head
Soon gave me to know
I had nothing to dread.

For Santa

He spoke not a word,
But went straight to his work
And filled all the stockings,
Then turned with a jerk.

And laying a finger
Aside of his nose,
And giving a nod,
Up the chimney he rose.

He sprang to his sleigh,
To his team gave a whistle,
And away they all flew
Like the down of a thistle.

But I heard him exclaim
Ere he drove out of sight,
"Happy Christmas to all.
And to all a good night."